Copyright © 2018 by Soothing Waterfalls Books
ISBN-13: 978-0-692-06438-2

Dedicated to the memory of my loving mother

Dr. Denise Treadwell Thompkins

Maya

and her
BEHAVIOR THERAPIST

By *A. D. Thompkins*

Illustrator *Hezekiah Johnson*

Hi! My name is Maya and I want to tell you all about me! I live with my mommy and my daddy and my brother. I am 5 years old and I'm in kindergarten. I have a cat, a dog, 10 goldfish, 3 turtles, and 2 birds.

My mommy tells me I'm a very special kid. She says that I have something called autism. I don't know what that means though. Mommy tells me I am just like any other kid, but I just do things a little differently than other kids my age.

Sometimes when I'm in school, the kids in my classroom can get really loud! It hurts my ears so much I have to cover them.

Covering my ears doesn't always help. Sometimes I just don't know what to do or what to say to get the noise to stop, so I just start screaming, fall to the floor, and kick my legs wildly. And when I scream, oh boy, I see my teacher Mrs. Wiggleby coming my way trying her hardest to calm me down.

I like going to the store with my mommy. There are so many cool things to look at! Sometimes I run away so I can get a closer look at the toys. Mommy tells me it is not safe to run away. She says that I am supposed to ask first and that a grown up should always be with me. But I can't help it. I'm just so excited to see the cool toys! I'm sad now because since I always run away from mommy, she doesn't take me to the store anymore.

I also like to eat, but I only like to eat one thing - chicken nuggets! If it were my choice I would eat chicken nuggets for breakfast, lunch, and dinner. I would even eat them for snack! And they must be warm. Not hot, not cold, but warm. And if they are not warm I will refuse to eat them! I love my warm chicken nuggets!

Oh, and I don't like vegetables. Mommy cooks them, but they are so yucky! I feel sick from just looking at them. When mommy tells me to take a bite, I feel like I'm going to throw up! I don't like how vegetables feels in my mouth. I don't like many fruits either. Bananas are the absolute worst! They're slimy and mushy, and gross! And if they have brown spots on the peel, I won't even touch them! Mommy says that eating chicken nuggets all the time is not healthy and that I must eat my fruits and vegetables, but I will not. They are all so disgusting!

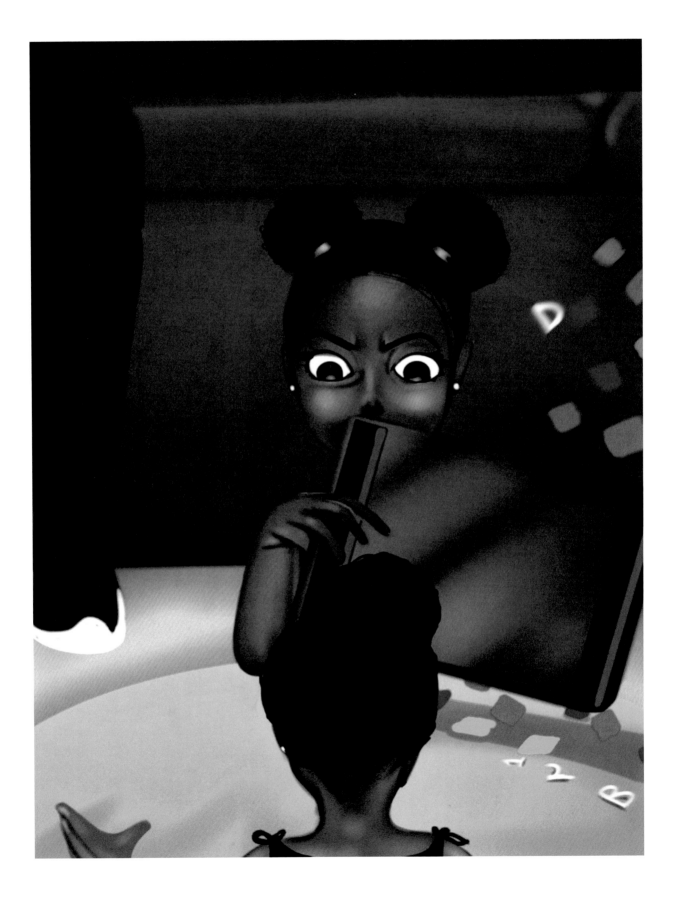

I like having friends too! Sometimes my friends stop being my friend. I like playing games with my friends, but I HATE losing! One day I was playing a game and my friend was about to win. I didn't like that, so I flipped the game board over! She is not my friend anymore. I had another friend that would always sit way too close to me when we watched cartoons. So, I would push her to get her away from me. She stopped being my friend too.

I had another friend I played dolls with, but she stopped being my friend because I always snatched toys out of her hand. I can't help it, I just wanted every toy she picked up. Mommy told me snatching is not nice and that I should ask first, but I always forget.

Sometimes mommy takes me to the playground where I can meet new friends. She tells me I should look at them and say hi. But I don't like looking in people's eyes. It makes me feel uncomfortable. I will tell you a little secret, but you can't tell mommy. When mommy tells me to look at someone in their eyes when I say hi, I never really look at their eyes. I look at their nose…ha ha ha ha!

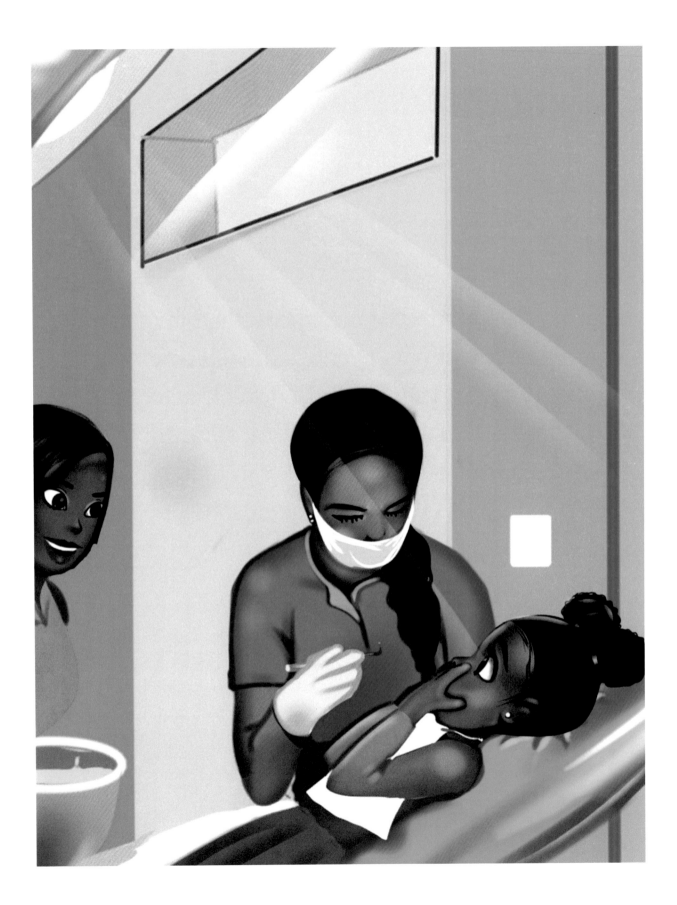

Oh, I forgot to tell you I love candy! I like lollipops, jelly beans, bubblegum, sweet tarts, caramel, candy bars, and licorice. Gummy bears and chocolate candies are my all-time favorite! Unfortunately, I get cavities and have to go to the dentist a lot! I hate going to the dentist! First, I have to sit in the lobby. Boring! They have toys to play with, but I don't want to play with them. I like climbing on the chairs, but mommy tells me to sit down.

Then they call mommy and I back and make me sit in a chair. Next to the chair they have all these weird tools they want to put in my mouth. No way! They might hurt. Mommy says that the dentist won't hurt me, but I don't believe her. Those tools look scary, shiny, and sharp! Now, since I never open my mouth and I cry and run away from the dentist, they give me medicine to make me sleep so they can fix my cavities.

Did I mention I love going to the beach? Building sand castles is so much fun! I also like playing in the water. One day me and my family went to the beach. We were there a long time, but it was time to go. We packed all our belongings and mommy told me to put on my shoes.

When I put my foot in my shoe I screamed so loud then I kicked my shoe off my foot. Mommy kept asking me what was wrong. But I just cried and screamed. I threw anything that I could get my hands on. Then I fell on the sand, rolled around and continued screaming! Daddy picked up my shoe and put it back on my foot. I screamed even louder and then kicked both of them off! Mommy took my little brother by the hand, picked up our belongings, daddy picked me up, and we left.

When we were in the car, mommy wasn't very happy with me. She said that I embarrassed her because I was screaming and crying. I felt bad about embarrassing my mommy. But what mommy didn't understand was that I don't like it when there is stuff in my shoes. That day it was sand. Another day, there was water in my shoes and I screamed as I did when I was at the beach, but mommy and daddy didn't know what was wrong. I just don't like when there are things in my shoes other than my feet! I wish they knew that.

When we got home, mommy made me take a bath and sent me to my room to take a nap.

When I got up she told me she wanted to help me improve my behavior. She said that she found someone who could help. She used very big words and said, "I found a Board-Certified Behavior Analyst to come and help you improve your behavior."

Mommy told me we would meet with the, the, the…I can't remember the big words, but I'll just call her my behavior therapist. Mommy said that the behavior therapist would be coming by to meet me. Well, mommy wasn't kidding. Ms. Cruz came to my house. Now, I can't get rid of her. She comes to my house after school on Mondays, Tuesdays, and Wednesdays! She stays for 2 hours each day! Can you believe that…two-whole-hours!

At first when she came to my house I screamed a lot. She tried to play with me, but I didn't want to play with her. I didn't follow directions when she told me to do things. If she said sit down, I continued standing. One time she told me to sit in a chair. I started crying and fell on the floor.

If she told me to come here, I ran in the opposite direction away from her. One time she asked me to draw a circle. I refused. Instead, I tore the paper in half and threw the pencil across the room. Then she told me to color neatly on a coloring sheet. Guess what I did? I scribble scrabbled all over the page coloring outside the lines using a black crayon! Another time she told me to write my name. I picked up the pencil, but I just sat there, stared at the paper, and never wrote my name.

I hated sitting at the table to work. I felt like I was in school even though I had just gotten out of school. But that changed. We didn't always sit at the table. Sometimes we'd work on the floor. That was fun! Sometimes we sat on the sofa in the living room and worked, and other times we worked at the dining room table. Oh, and I forgot about the time we worked in my backyard, but it was hard for me to concentrate so we had to come back in.

When I get things right, she gives me high fives and pats on the back. She tickled me once, but I don't like tickles. So, she just sticks with the high fives and pats on the back. Ms. Cruz always tells me exactly what I am doing right. For example, she tells me, "Maya, excellent job following directions by sitting down," or "Maya, you did a great job waiting with a quiet mouth!" Ms. Cruz is awesome! When she tells me nice things like that it makes me want to get even more things right and follow all of her directions!

And guess what else Ms. Cruz does that really helps me. Before we work Ms. Cruz draws a picture of everything that we will do. That's very nice. I don't like it when I don't know what will happen next. She even makes a board that says, "First, Then!" What this means is FIRST I have to work THEN I get to have fun! After I work appropriately I get to earn fun things like playing a game on the tablet. If I do really really well, I may even get two fun things like a small piece of my favorite candy and time to watch a few minutes of my favorite cartoon! Ms. Cruz is so cool!

Whew, I just finished playing soccer with my friends, but I wanted to tell you about another time I did extremely well by following my therapist's directions immediately. Immediately means I did what she asked me to do right away instead of when I felt like doing it.

Ms. Cruz told me to color neatly, then put my crayons back in the crayon box, and put my crayon box in my backpack. Well, I did all of those things. Boy, she was super excited! She picked me up, did a little spin and said, "Great job following all of the directions! I am so proud of you!" She put me down, gave me a high five, and a pat on the back. She then gave me free time to play with my dolls. She even played with me. She also gave me 2 gummy bears instead of one or a half of one and she gave me my favorite color gummy bear...the red ones! Yummy!

I like Ms. Cruz now. She's my best friend. Since I've been working with her, I have learned so much. I even made new friends and I'm keeping my friends. Ms. Cruz taught me that when people are too close to me, I can ask them nicely to give me space. Ms. Cruz also taught me about having good sportsmanship. That means being nice if someone else wins. She says I can say things like, 'good job' or 'way to go' when my friends win the game. She taught me that losing isn't so bad. Now when I play games with my friends losing isn't a big deal.

She even taught me something I can say when I don't want to put on my shoes because something is in it. I can say, 'mommy please wipe my feet' or mommy, there's something in my shoe, please take it out'. And guess who is eating vegetables now? Me!!! Ms. Cruz let me try vegetables that were raw…raw means not cooked. So, now I like broccoli, carrots, cauliflower, and celery. They are nice and crunchy! She said I could dip my celery in peanut butter, but I don't like that. She also said that I could dip my broccoli in ranch salad dressing. But I don't like that either. I just like my veggies plain.

You would be so proud of me because I am also eating fruits now! I tried eating a banana, but I really just don't like them. Ms. Cruz says that I don't have to eat bananas, because there are a lot of other fruits that I can try. Well now I like apples! I can eat a whole apple or apple slices. I also like mandarin oranges. And I love cherries, but I have to be careful because they have seeds in them. Strawberries and grapes are yummy too!

I could go on and on about how Ms. Cruz helps me, but I know you're probably getting tired of sitting and listening to this story. So, I want to tell all the kids around the world listening to my story or reading it yourself that if you have a behavior therapist, listen to them. They will never hurt you. They are only there to help you and they really really care about you. And if you need a reminder about how they can help you like they helped me, ask them to read this book to you. I'm sure it will help. Thanks for listening!

Made in the USA
Lexington, KY
10 June 2018